Granny's Little Rhyme Book

A COLLECTION OF FAVORITE NURSERY RHYMES

Illustrated by HENRIETTE WILLEBEEK LE MAIR

Philomel Books • *New York*

— ABOUT THE ILLUSTRATOR —

Henriette Willebeek le Mair was born in Rotterdam, Holland, in 1889 and had her first book, *Premiers Rondes Enfantines*, published in France when she was only fifteen. Ms. le Mair illustrated fourteen books in all between 1911 and 1926, including *Our Old Nursery Rhymes, Little Songs of Long Ago,* and *Gallery of Children* (all available in new Philomel editions).

Between 1911 and 1917, le Mair was the pre-eminent illustrator of her time and today her work exists mostly in private collections. She died in 1966.

Contents

Oranges and Lemons

Oranges and lemons,
Say the bells of St. Clement's.

You owe me five farthings,
Say the bells of St. Martin's.

When will you pay me?
Say the bells of Old Bailey.

When I grow rich,
Say the bells of Shoreditch.

When will that be?
Say the bells of Stepney.

I do not know,
Says the great bell at Bow.

Simple Simon

Simple Simon met a pieman,
    Going to the fair;
Says Simple Simon to the pieman,
    Let me taste your ware.

Says the pieman to Simple Simon,
    Show me first your penny;
Says Simple Simon to the pieman,
    Indeed I have not any.

Simple Simon went a-fishing,
    For to catch a whale;
All the water he had got
    Was in his mother's pail.

Simple Simon went to look
    If plums grew on a thistle;
He pricked his finger very much,
    Which made poor Simon whistle.

He went to catch a dickey bird,
    And thought he could not fail;
Because he'd got a little salt,
    To put upon its tail.

He went for water in a sieve,
    But soon it ran all through;
And now poor Simple Simon
    Bids you all adieu.

I Saw Three Ships

I saw three ships come sailing by,
　　Come sailing by, come sailing by,
I saw three ships come sailing by,
　　On New-Year's day in the morning.

And what do you think was in them then,
　　Was in them then, was in them then?
And what do you think was in them then,
　　On New-Year's day in the morning?

Three pretty girls were in them then,
　　Were in them then, were in them then,
Three pretty girls were in them then,
　　On New-Year's day in the morning.

One could whistle, and one could sing,
　　And one could play on the violin;
Such joy there was at my wedding,
　　On New-Year's day in the morning.

Jack and Jill

Jack and Jill went up the hill
    To fetch a pail of water;
Jack fell down and broke his crown,
    And Jill came tumbling after.
Up Jack got, and home did trot,
    As fast as he could caper,
To old Dame Dob, who patched his nob
    With vinegar and brown paper.

Little Boy Blue

Little Boy Blue,
    Come blow your horn,
The sheep's in the meadow,
    The cow's in the corn;
But where is the boy
    Who looks after the sheep?
He's under a haystack
    Fast asleep.
Will you wake him?
    No, not I,
    For if I do, he's sure to cry.

Pat-a-Cake

Pat-a-cake, pat-a-cake, baker's man,
 Bake me a cake as fast as you can;
Pat it and prick it, and mark it with **B**,
 Put it in the oven for baby and me.

Goosey, Goosey, Gander

Goosey, goosey gander,
    Whither shall I wander?
Upstairs and downstairs
    And in my lady's chamber.
There I met an old man
    Who would not say his prayers.
I took him by the left leg
    And threw him down the stairs.

Lavender's Blue

Lavender's blue, dilly, dilly,
 Lavender's green;
When I am king, dilly, dilly,
 You shall be queen.

Call up your men, dilly, dilly,
 Set them to work,
Some to the plough, dilly, dilly,
 Some to the cart.

Some to make hay, dilly, dilly,
 Some to thresh corn,
Whilst you and I, dilly, dilly,
 Keep ourselves warm.

Lucy Locket

Lucy Locket lost her pocket,
Kitty Fisher found it;
Not a penny was there in it,
Only a ribbon round it.

Georgie Porgie

Georgie Porgie, pudding and pie,
  Kissed the girls and made them cry;
When the boys came out to play,
  Georgie Porgie ran away.

Copyright © 1990 by Soefi Stichting Inayat Fundatie Sirdar.
Published in The United States in 1990 by Philomel Books,
a division of The Putnam & Grosset Group,
200 Madison Avenue, New York, 10016. Published simultaneously in Canada.
Originally published by Gallery Children's Books, an imprint of
East-West Publications (UK) Ltd., London. All rights reserved
Printed in Hong Kong by South China Printing Co. (1988) Ltd.
Library of Congress Catalouing-in-Publication Data
Willebeek le Mair, H. (Henriette), 1889 – 1966.
Granny's little rhyme book/by Henriette Willebeek le Mair.   p.   cm.
Summary: An illustrated collection of ten nursery rhymes, including
"Oranges and Lemons," "Little Boy Blue," and "Lucy Locket."
1. Nursery rhymes. 2. Children's poetry. [1. Nursery rhymes.]
I. Title. PZ8.3.W6686Au 1990   398.8--dc20   89-23066 CIP
ISBN 0-399-22174-3
First impression